MW00943024

Maine ABC

Susan Ramsay Hoguet

For Abigail, Suzannah, Ashley, Peter, and Courtney with love

A is for alewives in Damariscotta Mills.

B is for a bear in the Camden Hills.

C is for a chickadee on the branch of a pine.

D is a dory hauled up with a line.

E is an eagle alone in flight.

F is for fiddleheads curled up tight.

G is for gulls, the fisherman's bane.

H is for halibut in the Gulf of Maine.

I is for islands, some big and some small.

J is a Jack-in-the-pulpit, twelve inches tall.

K is for Katahdin with snow at the top.

L is for lobster escaping the pot.

M is for moose in a Greenville bog.

N is for newt out from under a log.

O is an osprey nest of twigs from a tree.

P is for puffins living on islands and sea.

Q is for quahog, whose bottom's like its top.

R is for rabbit, who moves with a hop.

S is for seal, quite slippery when wet.

T is for trout in a lake near Lubec.

U is for an urchin shell washed up in a gale.

V is for vole, a mouse with a short tail.

W is for a whale in Frenchman Bay.

X is a crossing sign, a warning each way.

Y is for yawl, whose masts stand tall.

Then, what do you see?

A zillion snowflakes for the letter **Z**.

ISBN 978-1-60893-182-8

Design by Rich Eastman

Printed in China
5 4 3 2 1

Distributed to the trade by National Book Network

Library of Congress Cataloging-in-Publication
information available upon request.